To Peter, who supplies the love

Library of Congress Catalog Card number: 98-89229   ISBN: 0-307-10228-9   MM

The illustrations in this book were cut from origami paper and found paper, such as envelopes, bags, and homemade fiber paper. The shapes were cut with Scherenschnitte scissors and pasted in position with a glue stick and a pair of tweezers.

SNOW

written & illustrated by
Nancy Elizabeth Wallace

A Golden Book • New York
Golden Books Publishing Company, Inc.
New York, New York 10106

I have always loved the snow.

When I was small, my brother Max and I lived where the meadow meets the wood. Each winter morning I looked out the window, hoping that a blanket of white had covered the earth during the night.

On gray winter days, Max and I often watched from the green bench by the window. Whoever saw the first flakes drifting down would shout, "It's snowing!"

Then our mama would help us bundle up in
snow pants and jackets and scarves and boots.
We squiggled and squirmed to hurry outside.

I remember that Max and I would stick out our tongues to catch snowflakes. We could taste their coldness. Sometimes, if we were very careful, we might catch one, single, perfect flake to look at.

It is still a wonder to me that each and every snowflake, in all of time, is different.

On the fresh new snow in the meadow, we would lie down and make prints with our bodies. I remember saying, "Hush, Max, be still." And for a moment or two we lay there listening to the silence.

One time Max and I rolled up small snowballs
until they grew bigger and bigger and bigger.

We piled one on top of another
and sculpted snow ears. Our mama gave
us her old pink scarf to tie around the
snow rabbit's neck. She laughed.
"I think it looks like Grandpa."

Max insisted that we leave a carrot
for our snow rabbit in case he got
hungry during the night.

When we came back to visit the next day,
there were nibble marks on the carrot.

This is true.

Max and I had a sled made of birchwood.
We would pull it up to the top of the hill.
Then down, down we slid to the bottom,
gliding on two runners, leaving a trail
behind.

Max would always say, "I want to be
in front. Let me be in front."

Most times I would.

Whenever the ground was covered with snow, we would sprinkle sunflower seeds to feed the birds.

Our mama said, "If we start to feed the birds in winter, we must continue until spring because they will come to depend on us."

So we did.

Afterward, in our snug kitchen, we made
hot chocolate. Max liked to measure out
the six spoonfuls of cocoa.

"One, two, three, four, five, six," he'd count.

I, because I was older, poured the milk. Then
Mama heated it on the stove, adding a little
bit of honey. We would all drink in the warmness.

Though many years have gone by,
I still feel the magic when it snows.